Dear _Audrey_

Please join us for

Tea Time

Much love,

Sophia Grace and Rosie

Love,
Grammy

_2015_

Tea
with Sophia

Time
Grace and Rosie

BY SOPHIA GRACE BROWNLEE AND ROSIE McCLELLAND

AS TOLD TO ORLI ZURAVICKY

ILLUSTRATED BY SHELAGH McNICHOLAS

ORCHARD BOOKS / NEW YORK / AN IMPRINT OF SCHOLASTIC INC.

This magical book is dedicated to all little princesses everywhere. This delightful story was inspired by Sophia Grace and Rosie's innocent imagination captured through play. From fairies to princesses, fairy dust to wands, join us on a magical journey. Every little girl dreams of being a princess, and Sophia Grace and Rosie's adventure brings this to life.

From Sophia Grace and her family:

We would like to say a big thank you to *The Ellen DeGeneres Show*, Warner Bros., and Telepictures — and a special thank you to David McGuire of Telepictures. Thank you to Kara Hogan Leonardo. A big thank you to Bonnie, Meghan, Rebecca, Susan, and all at PYE. A special thank you to Sophia Grace's idols, Nicki Minaj and Ellen DeGeneres, for making her dreams come true. Thank you to attorneys Darrell Thompson and Fabian Milburn, both trusted friends. Thank you to Shelagh McNicholas, the talented illustrator, and Orli Zuravicky. Thank you to Orchard Books and Scholastic for making this book possible. Thank you to the best hype girl in the world, cousin Rosie. Thank you to Sylvia Young and Julie and all at the Sylvia Young Agency. A special thank you to Sophia Grace's school for their ongoing support.

Sophia Grace would like to send hugs and kisses and a very special thank you to her mummy, Carly, and daddy, Dominic, for coming along on this magical journey.

From Rosie and her family:

We would like to say a big sparkly Thank You to Rosie's management at PYE, Patty Mayer, Ellen DeGeneres, Kara Hogan Leonardo, everyone at *The Ellen DeGeneres Show*, Telepictures, David McGuire, and Nicki Minaj. We would also like to thank Headteacher Mr. Tye.

Rosie would like to send a special thank you to her cousin, Sophia Grace, for this amazing journey they are on together and most of all her mummy and daddy, Danielle and Greg, for their love and support. "Love you up to the moon and back."

Mummy Danielle and Daddy Greg would like to say thank you to their precious Princess Rosie for all the happiness she brings them and for making their lives truly complete.

"Let's have a tea party tomorrow!"

Sophia Grace and Rosie just *loved*
having tea parties!
In fact, the two cousins had already
thrown several of them.
Some were for famous
singers or movie stars.
Others were just for
family or friends.

By now the girls were
experts in every kind of
tea party imaginable!

"I'm *so* excited!" Rosie replied. "Who shall we invite this time?"

"I've got it!" exclaimed Sophia Grace. "We each get to invite one *really* special person."

"Someone we love more than anyone else!" Rosie jumped up and down in agreement.

"And we'll surprise each other," Sophia Grace added. "This is going to be *so* good!"

The two girls clapped their hands with excitement and set off to plan their party.

"Let's write out the invitations," Rosie said.

They each took a piece of pink paper, of course, and carefully wrote what they wanted to say.

Then they decorated their invitations with flowers, princess stickers, and gold glitter glue so they would sparkle. After all, everything really is better with glitter glue!

"This invitation is *so* pretty!" exclaimed Sophia Grace. "Do you know who you are inviting yet?"

"No, not yet," Rosie answered. "Do you?"

"No," Sophia Grace replied. "But the person I invite *has* to love pink as much as I do!"

"Me, too!" replied Rosie. "She should love sparkles, as well."

"Oh, yes!" Sophia Grace agreed. "Also, she'll need to love dressing up as much as we do."

Rosie nodded enthusiastically.

Next the girls turned their attention to discussing the theme of the tea party.

The Grammys?

Chocolate?

Fairies?

California?

Cotton Candy?

Pink!

Fairy dust makes everything magical!

And messy . . .

"Where shall we have our party this time?" Sophia Grace asked.

"What about Disneyland?" Rosie offered.

"Disneyland is *so* good!" Sophia Grace agreed.

"*So* good! But isn't it far away?" Rosie asked.

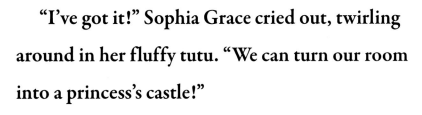

"I've got it!" Sophia Grace cried out, twirling around in her fluffy tutu. "We can turn our room into a princess's castle!"

"I love that *so* much!" Rosie agreed.

"But how are we going to turn our room into a castle?" Rosie asked.

"I have an idea — but we'll need to ask our favorite fairies for help," Sophia Grace added. "It's *really* important for the party."

Rosie knew precisely what her cousin meant.

The girls closed their eyes, held hands, and called on their magical fairy friends.

When they opened their eyes, they were each holding a very special fairy wand.

"My party guest is going to love fairies as much as I do!" Rosie announced.

With the help of their magical fairy wands, the girls began turning their bedposts into majestic pillars, a bedside lamp into a crystal chandelier, and a nightstand into a golden glass table and chairs.

In no time they had transformed their bedroom into the
fanciest, most sparkly castle that ever existed!

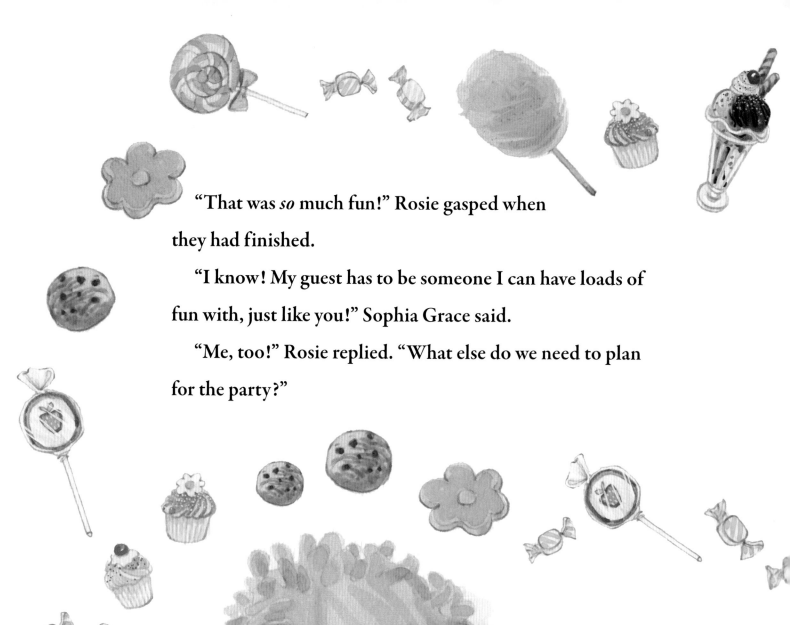

"That was *so* much fun!" Rosie gasped when they had finished.

"I know! My guest has to be someone I can have loads of fun with, just like you!" Sophia Grace said.

"Me, too!" Rosie replied. "What else do we need to plan for the party?"

"The menu!" Sophia Grace cried out. "Let's have a million different flavors of cotton candy!"

"And chocolate, lots of chocolate!" Rosie added. "Oh, and cookies."

"Our guests better love sweets as much as we do!" Sophia Grace replied.

"Sophia Grace," Rosie began as the two sat down to have a snack.

Planning a tea party was hard work, and their tummies were rumbling!

"Have you decided who your guest will be yet?"

"I think so," Sophia Grace replied, taking a bite out of her sandwich. "I know who I like spending time with more than anyone else in the world."

"Me, too," Rosie agreed, taking a sip from her juice box. "I can't wait till you find out who my guest is — you're going to be so surprised!"

"I feel exactly the same way."

The last step was deciding on the PERFECT tea party outfits.

Of course the girls absolutely had to try on every tutu they owned!

"You look lovely in blue," said Rosie.

"Ooh, that one really suits you!" Sophia Grace admired Rosie's pretty purple tutu and matching top.

"Pink is perfect," they both agreed.

"Boy, am I tired!" Sophia Grace said, letting out a huge yawn.

"Me, too," Rosie admitted, tucking herself under her covers.

"Goodnight, Princess Sophia Grace!"

"Goodnight, Princess Rosie."

That night, when each girl thought the other was sleeping,
she slipped out from under her covers, tiptoed over to her cousin's
bed, and hid something very special under her pillow.

Bright and early the next morning, the girls each awoke to
a lovely surprise.

Dear Sophia Grace,
You are cordially invited to
Tea Time with Rosie. Please
wear your tiara and fluffiest tutu.
I Love you!
Rosie x
p.s. Tea will be served on Sunday at 4 o'clock
in the afternoon in Sophia Grace and Rosie Castle

Dear Rosie,
You are cordially invited to
Tea Time with Sophia Grace.
Please wear your tiara and fluffiest tutu.
You are my hype girl!
I LOVE YOU!
Sophia Grace
p.s. Tea will be served on Sunday at 4 o'clock
in the afternoon in Sophia Grace and Rosie Castle

"This tea party is *so* good!" Sophia Grace exclaimed, chewing on her favorite flavor cotton candy.

"I know!" agreed Rosie. "Um, do you think we should return the wands to our fairies soon?" Rosie continued, taking a bite out of a flower cookie.

"I think we should hold on to them for a bit, just in case," Sophia Grace answered.

"I'm so glad it's just the two of us," Rosie said.

"Me, too," Sophia Grace answered. "Just the two of us. Sophia Grace and Rosie, rising to the top!"

Tea Tip 3

Make sure everyone has their own pretty place to sit with a pretty cup!

Tea Tip 4

Serve your favorite snacks and treats. It's fun to pretend.

To Mark, for your love, support, and dedication — S.M.